To Audrey,

Happy Reading!

Janice B

Tellwell Talent
www.tellwell.ca

ISBN
978-0-2288-9080-5 (Paperback)

BODHI THE ADVENTURER

Janice Breckon & Christina Amarilli

Thank you to our families for all their love, support and encouragement.

Bodhi was so excited that he couldn't sleep. In the morning, he was moving to the country to become a gardener.

Their family apartment was perfect for city life, but it had no space for a garden.

Bodhi just knew that in the country, he could grow everything he had ever dreamed of.

Bodhi woke up bright and early and zoomed through his breakfast before rushing upstairs to start packing.

Checklist:
Flashlight ☐
Toothbrush ☑
Sunscreen ☑

He had had his list ready for two weeks and knew exactly what he was going to take.

Momma gave Bodhi a bag of his favourite cookies,
and squeezed him tight.

He waved goodbye to his family
and left to catch his bus.

He sure was going to miss them.

"Yay, the bus, the bus, it's finally here!" Bodhi cheered.

He couldn't wait to start his new adventure!

Bodhi thought being on a bus was fantastic! He liked the soft squishy seats and the weird bus smells.

Everything swooshed by so quickly.

Bodhi was so happy to be in the country, it was everything he had ever imagined.

He pushed the bell and hopped off the bus.

Eager to start his garden, he skipped away down the road, singing his favourite song...

Bodhi soon came across a little mound of dirt.

"What a lovely spot for my garden", he thought. Taking out his shovel, he dug in with great gusto.

Home Sweet Home!

"I'm sorry little ants, I didn't see you there."

The next morning, Bodhi thought for sure he had found another good spot.

But, that didn't work out either.

"Sorrrrryyyyyyyyyy" he yelled as he ran
away from all the angry, nesting birds.

On the fourth day, things got even worse.

Poor Bodhi.

Bodhi had looked and looked and hadn't been able to find a spot for his garden anywhere and now, his shovel was broken too.

He was feeling sad and tired and he was starting to wonder if he had made the right choice by moving to the country.

HOOOo..

It was getting late, so Bodhi set up camp for another night in the forest.

He was missing his family a lot but when he heard the melodies of the crickets chirping and the owls hooing in the trees, he realized he wasn't alone after all.

The next morning, Bodhi woke up feeling much better. Finding a place for his garden would take some time, but that was okay.

After all, special things are worth it.

Bodhi came across
a lake and stopped to take a drink.

"Eeeek!" he sqeaked when he saw his
reflection. "What would Momma say if she
could see me now?". He had never ever
been so dirty in his whole life!

He laughed out loud
and dove in.

Bodhi was drying off, when he looked up and saw a bird with a caterpillar on its back.

"Hi! My name is Daisy Scarlett Rose," called out the caterpillar. "I was named after the two flowers I was born between.

This here is Hamish and he's my best friend.

What's your name? What are you doing? I'm hungry. Do you have anything to eat?"

"Hi, my name's Bodhi! I'm a gardener from the city. I've been looking for a spot to grow my garden, but I can't seem to find one anywhere. I hope to find it soon though, because I'm really getting tired of sleeping outside.

Here, Daisy Scarlett Rose. you can have some of my cookies".

"Thank you," Daisy Scarlett Rose replied, "Hamish and I love cookies. By the way, call me DD, everyone else does."

Just then, Hamish thought of a good idea.

"Wow, Hamish, that's a super-duper good idea!" DD blurted out. "Bodhi, you could come and stay with us at Roseberry Manor! Hamish and I live there and it's like a big, fancy campground-park. Everyone is welcome at the Manor!"

"Oh, that would be wonderful! I'd love to come"

"Ta-Da! We're heeeere!" DD said. "Just wait at the gate and the shuttle truck will bring you in.

We are going to go home now, Hamish is tired and wants to take a nap.

We'll catch up with you later, okay?

See you soon raccoon!"

The shuttle truck arrived at the front
gate and stopped for Bodhi to jump in.
He couldn't believe how full it was!

It parked behind a big, old manor house
and everybody piled off with excitement.

"Thank you, Mr. Shuttle Truck Driver" they all sang out.

Checking his Roseberry Manor map,
Bodhi went to investigate the cabins.

After searching for a while, Bodhi found a little cabin that was just right.

"Yay! No more sleeping outside!" he cheered.

He was unpacking all of his things, when
he felt his tummy rumble.

"Oh my! It must be time for dinner! I hope Hamish
and DD will be there"

Bodhi grabbed his map, and raced out the door
to find the kitchen.

Bodhi found the kitchen with no trouble at all.

He had never seen so many veggies before
and he couldn't wait to try them all.

"Bodhi! Over here! We saved you a seat,"
he heard DD calling out.

Later that night, Bodhi lay in bed satisfied with his long, eventful day. Even though he hadn't found a spot for his garden yet, he had found Roseberry Manor, DD and Hamish and they were all pretty amazing.

"What an adventure this had turned out to be", he thought.

Sending love to his family back home, he soon fell asleep looking forward to tomorrow.

After all, he still had a garden to find, and plant, and grow.

THE END

~ SEARCH & FIND ~

Three Little Bumble Bees

These three bumble bees are for Janice's three children, Rhianna, Tyler & Claire.

Find them on every page!

Where's Stevie?

Stevie is a white, fluffy cat that lives at Roseberry Manor. He is very curious and likes to explore.

Did you see Stevie?

The Field Mice

These two mice are Christina's nieces, Lily and Olivia. Like Stevie, they too live at Roseberry Manor and they're always together.

Look for them around the Manor!